Franziska Macur

Charlie & Noel
An Advent Calendar Story

Charlie & Noel – An Advent Calendar Story
Copyright Franziska Macur, 2013
www.homenaturally.org

Illustrations by Meghan Klaassen

Introduction

Simply Advent!

The Advent season is one of the most magical times of the year for me. It's a time of preparation, anticipation, and connection. It's a season when the smell of cookies is in the air. A season spent drinking hot chocolate with family and friends. The (sometimes frosty) air is filled with sparkles. The trees and houses are brightly decorated. And at night, thousands of lights shimmer in our neighborhood.

However, the Advent season can also be a time of stress, impatience, and exhaustion. It can quickly turn into a bad dream if you are stretched to your limit and unsure about how to meet all of the expectations that come with the Holidays. Even for children, the magic can sometimes fade. Instead of standing in awe before the Christmas tree, delighting in the sound of the Christmas songs or rejoicing in all of the little surprises that Advent has to offer, children can feel conflicted by contradicting messages of consumerism on the one hand, and what Christmas is really about on the other.

This Advent calendar story is designed to help you and your children travel mindfully through the Advent season. You will get to know Charlie, a little boy who wishes he could just skip the whole waiting part and jump right into the presents. But Charlie doesn't realize what he would be missing or just how many magical moments the season has waiting for him.

In this Advent season, put aside some quiet family time, read one short chapter, and talk about some of the issues raised by the story with your children. At the end of each Advent day, you'll also find discussion starters and ideas for additional activities. Join us in our journey, enjoy some precious time with the people you love most, and travel thoughtfully through this wonderful season together.

Happy Advent!

Warmly,
Franziska

Table of Contents

December 1 – Advent Begins

Just a few days after Thanksgiving, Charlie's cousins, his aunt, and his grandparents left after staying with them for the long weekend. It was fun to have them around. But it was also fun to have all his toys back to himself. Well, not quite. He needed to share a little with his sister Isabelle. But she was only one, so pretty much a baby. Charlie was already six.

"Hey, Charlie," his dad called, "Do you want to go down to the basement with me and get the Christmas tree?"

Charlie's eyes lit up. "Is it Christmas, yet?" he asked.

His dad laughed. "Not quite. But tomorrow begins the season of Advent and I would like to start decorating the house."

Charlie kicked one of his Legos. The block hit the pile of toys in the middle of the play room. "Advent is stupid,"

Charlie mumbled. He pulled out his self-destructing tank from the toy pile and tried to find the missing parts to assemble it.

His dad sighed. "Well, if you change your mind, you know where you can find me."

Charlie pretended to be busy with his tank.

One hour later, the tree was set up. His mom took ornaments out of boxes while his dad assembled a little stable for the nativity scene. Isabelle was playing with Baby Jesus. Charlie looked at all the decorations. It looked pretty. Oh, he so wished it would be Christmas right now! But even the chocolate Advent calendars that his grandpa dropped off for Charlie and Isabelle couldn't lift Charlie's mood.

"At Christmas," he thought, "there will be much more chocolate!"

Charlie went back to the living room after dinner. All the boxes were put away and his mom had even put a few presents under the tree. Charlie was trying to figure out which one was for him. He picked each one up, shook it, and tried to read the name tags when he noticed a little plush donkey sitting under the tree next to the presents. The donkey seemed to look at him. Charlie put the present quickly back under the tree. "What was going on?" he thought.

Family talk – December 1

1. What does Advent mean? What does it mean to you and your family?
   - ➤ Noun
     - The arrival of a notable person, thing, or event.
     - The first season of the church year, leading up to Christmas and including the four preceding Sundays.
   - ➤ Synonyms
     - Coming
     - Arrival
     - Appearance
2. Why is it so hard to wait sometimes?
3. Further things to do: Make an Advent wreath or Advent craft
   http://goo.gl/1o1Ryd

December 2 – The Donkey

Charlie checked on the donkey in the morning but wasn't quite sure what to do.

"Is it time for breakfast, yet?" he asked his mom.

"In about ten minutes," she replied. "You have some time to play."

Charlie paced between the kitchen and the living room, every so often risking a peak toward the tree. The donkey was still sitting there . . . looking at him. Charlie went back to the kitchen and offered to set the table.

But eventually curiosity won and Charlie went back to the tree after breakfast.

"Okay," he said to the donkey, "what's going on?"

The donkey looked at him somewhat amused. "Don't you remember me?" he asked Charlie.

Charlie studied the donkey. He vaguely

remembered something but he didn't exactly know what it was. He shook his head.

The donkey sighed. "I was one of your Christmas presents last year," he said. "But you never really looked at me so I went and lived in the basement. I figured since you are a year older, we might be friends now."

Charlie's eyes got big. "You mean like an early Christmas present?" he asked.

The donkey shook his head. "No, Charlie. It's not Christmas yet. It's Advent. Advent is the time to get ready for Christmas. It's a wonderful and magical time. But I heard that you are not really that thrilled about Advent, right?"

Charlie nodded.

"Well, what would you think about travelling through Advent with me this year?"

Charlie hesitated for a second. He still thought that whoever thought of Advent had come up with a very dumb idea. But there wasn't anything he could do about it now, so he sighed and nodded. Advent couldn't be that hard if you had a talking donkey with you, right?

"Come back tomorrow," the donkey said.

"Okay," said Charlie. "One more question: Can I show you to my family?"

"You can show me to them but they won't be able to talk to me," smiled the donkey. "I was your present, remember?"

Family talk – December 2

1. Why do you think the donkey talked to Charlie?
2. Why does the donkey emphasize the difference between Advent and Christmas?
3. Further things to do: Make a donkey. http://goo.gl/iDw75F

December 3 – The Christmas List

Charlie got around cleaning-up after dinner and went to sit by the Christmas tree next to the donkey.

"What are you up to today, Charlie?" asked the donkey.

"I'm writing my Christmas list." Charlie said, his eyes filling with excitement. There was marker all over his hands, so the donkey knew that Charlie had already worked on it for quite a while.

"What did you write down?" asked the donkey.

"Well," said Charlie, "I just started and I looked through that big book that came in the mail…. you know, the one with all the toys in it? There is so much cool stuff in it! But mommy said I can only write one page because Santa doesn't have enough time to read more than one page. So I have to choose which things I really want… and I have to write in really small letters."

The donkey smiled and listened.

"But, you know," Charlie continued, "everybody is getting one of those marshmallow action figures for Christmas this year – Marcus even gets two. So I better put that on the list, for sure."

"Do you like them?" asked the donkey.

"Well, duh. Everybody likes them. They are super-cool." Charlie looked puzzled at the donkey.

"I understand," said the donkey. "But how do you play with them?"

Charlie hesitated: "You have them, and show them to others, and, hmmm, you, you, you fight each other's figures!" Now he looked triumphantly at the donkey.

"Charlie?" asked the donkey. "Do me a favor and take some time with your list, ok? Sleep on it for a few more nights and then maybe bring it back here in a few days?"

Charlie wrinkled his nose. "Fine," he said.

He got up from the floor and started to take a few steps. Then he turned around. "Hey donkey? I don't know what your name is."

The donkey smiled. "I was *your* present. You need to name me."

Charlie went slowly back into the kitchen.

Family talk – December 3

1. Have you and/or your kids written a Christmas list yet? How did you approach it?
2. Further (fun and thought-provoking) reading for parents:
http://goo.gl/giapm2

December 4 – Barbara Branches

Charlie was getting ready to go to school. He was trying to find his mittens and hat in time so he wouldn't miss the bus, which was already late. Then he heard the donkey call.

"What is it?" he asked with a hushed voice. "I'm really late."

He heard his mom in the kitchen. "Charlie, did you call me? You really need to go. Let me run upstairs and get your other hat."

"Charlie," said the donkey in a very quiet voice, "did you know that today, some people celebrate a woman named Barbara who lived a long, long time ago?"

Charlie shook his head.

"So do me a favor and when you have some time at school, look up her story."

"Fine," said Charlie. "Anything else?"

"Well, since you asked, bring home a branch from a cherry tree, too." The donkey smiled.

Charlie just shook his head. He took the hat from his mom and ran to the door. Turning, he ran back one more time to hug his mom and out the door he was.

It was already getting dark when Charlie came home.

"What is this?" asked his mom, pointing at the branch Charlie was carrying.

"It's from a cherry tree. Because of Barbara day," Charlie replied. He sneaked a peek at the donkey, who was pretending to sleep under the tree. But Charlie knew he was listening.

"Tell me more about Barbara. Did you talk about her today?" asked his mom.

"Well, kind of," said Charlie. "Barbara was a young woman who lived a long, long time ago and had to die because of her Christian faith. The story says that on her way to prison, a cherry branch got tangled in her dress. She put it in water and it bloomed the day she was executed. It means that since the dead branch bloomed again, that Barbara was not afraid to die, but she was thinking of eternal life, whatever that means." Charlie rattled off the information as fast as he could, worried that he would forget something.

"That's beautiful, Charlie," said his mom. "Let's put the branch in the special vase that we got from your great-grandma. Maybe it will bloom on Christmas. That would be a very special present, wouldn't it?"

Charlie's mom put the branch carefully on the counter and went to get the vase. Charlie looked at the donkey. He still pretended to sleep but Charlie knew that he had listened the whole time...

Family talk – December 4

1. If you have time, go outside and gather some branches. If there is no cherry tree nearby, some people also use apple, chestnut, pear, peach, forsythia, plum, lilac or jasmine branches.
2. What does the branch mean? How does this align with the message of Advent?
3. Further reading for parents: http://goo.gl/TqYvdt

December 5 – What's in a Name?

Charlie sat down next to the donkey.

"I brought a list," he said proudly.

"Oh," said the donkey, "you revised your Christmas list?"

"No," Charlie sighed, "I'm still working on that. But I made a list with possible names for you."

The donkey looked excited: "Let's hear them."

"Well, first I thought of Dodo. Just because it sounds good, you know. Dodo the Donkey."

The donkey did not look amused.

"But then I figured that you need a more meaningful name; something that actually has something to do with Advent and Christmas and all that stuff."

The donkey nodded and Charlie could see that he was intrigued.

"So I thought first about Jesus. That seemed to make sense because Christmas is all about Jesus, right? But then I figured that you are sitting right next to Baby Jesus in the manger and that would be kind of confusing…"

The donkey agreed.

"My second idea was to name you Gabriel. You know, after the angel that came to Mary? I still think it's a good name, and if you want to you have it, you can, but it does sound very serious… Not sure if that's the right name for a donkey."

The donkey wrinkled his forehead. "I can be very serious," he said.

"Oh, yes, of course", said Charlie. "I didn't mean it like that. However, my last idea was to name you Noel. You know? It means Christmas. And it sounds so nice. And I think it just fits perfectly!" Charlie beamed and looked at the donkey with great expectation. "So….?"

The donkey bobbed his head slowly back and forth. A big smile spread across his face. "It's perfect," he said.

Family talk – December 5

1. What does your name mean?
2. Why did your parents pick it for you?
3. Further things to do: Do a Christmas tree name craft.

   http://goo.gl/2p6rdA

December 6 – Nicholas

Before washing his face or brushing his teeth, Charlie ran to the front door. He pulled it open and stared at his boots. There they were, neatly standing in front of the door, right next to his sister's boots. Charlie looked inside; they looked empty. But that couldn't be. It was Nicholas day, after all. You were supposed to have something in your shoes….some candy…or maybe even a little toy. At least, that's what grandpa told him.

Charlie held the boots upside down and shook them. A tiny letter fell out. Charlie ripped it open and pulled out a note. It said:

Charlie was confused and disappointed. No candy, no toys, only a note that didn't make any sense.

"What's up with you this morning?" Noel asked.

Charlie showed him the note.

Noel looked at it for a while and then grinned.

"I know," Noel said. "It's about the story of Saint Nicholas. Many people, especially in Europe, celebrate this day because he was a role model for living a compassionate life. Nicholas' wealthy parents died when he was still young. Obeying Jesus' words to "sell what you own and give the money to the poor," Nicholas used his whole inheritance to assist the needy, the sick, and the suffering. He dedicated his life to serving God and was made Bishop of Myra while still a young man. Bishop Nicholas became known throughout the land for his generosity to those in need, for his love of children, and for his concern of sailors and ships." Noel looked very content and smiled at Charlie. "I always liked the story of Nicholas," he said.

Charlie wrinkled his nose impatiently. "Well, that's all really cool," he said, "but what does this have to do with the note?"

"Ah, right," Noel nodded. "I think I might have an idea, but we have to wait and see what happens today."

Charlie made a grumpy face and stomped off to the kitchen.

When he came home from school, his mom was waiting for him at the door, looking excited. "Charlie, you got mail!" Charlie didn't even take his shoes or coat off. He opened the letter and read:

Dear Charlie,

    Thank you for sending your
Nicholas sweets to the children
in our hospital. We were all so
excited when we got the note from
Nicholas explaining that you shared
them with us. Please come and
visit us when you have time.
We would love to meet you.

                The children from
                        Floor 4B

Family talk - December 6

1. Did you ever experience something where you know somebody must have intervened but you never found out who?

2. Further things to do: Send a Thank You card to somebody who did something nice for you.

December 7 – Ideas

Charlie was still beaming from the letter when he woke up the next morning.

"How many sweets do you think Nicholas brought them," he asked his dad.

"Not sure," he replied. "But it must have been a lot if there was enough for the whole floor."

Charlie thought hard, "Do you think grandpa told them? I mean, I never said anything about it to him, but maybe he just knew that this would be so cool. Do you think we could do that again next year? Maybe I could go with Nicholas…When do you think we can go and visit those kids? Should we bring them something else?"

Charlie couldn't stop wondering, asking questions, and just glowing about this mysterious and awesome happening. And in school his best friend even shared his chocolate with him when he heard

Charlie's story. It was just too good.

His dad looked at him and smiled, "Maybe you could think about giving them something for Christmas. For instance, you could write them a card and bake cookies?"

Charlie took the letter to Noel after breakfast and told him all about what had happened. Noel listened patiently and shared in Charlie's festive mood.

"Dad said I should send them a card or make cookies for Christmas," Charlie said to Noel. "But I think they need something much cooler. I wish I could buy them all a marshmallow action figure!"

Noel shook his head slowly. "That might be cool, Charlie, but sometimes we can make people's day with things that cost much less money. I have a feeling you will come up with a great idea if you just give it day or so."

Charlie nodded. But he was about to go ice skating with his family, so he didn't have tons of time to think about it.

"I'll write it on a post-it note over my bed," he said to Noel. "That way I won't forget!"

Family talk – December 7

1. Come up with an unusual idea on how to make somebody's (Christmas) day.
2. Further things to do: Draw or build a marshmallow action figure.

December 8 – The List, Again

Charlie was playing with his cars when his mom called. "Charlie," she said, "Aunt Sarah asked for your Christmas list. Do you want to go over it with me?"

"It's not ready yet," Charlie replied. "Can I have another day? It's just…well, mom, do you think I can put them in order? Like number one is what I really, really want and number thirty is what's just okay?"

His mom was silent for a while. Then she spoke very quietly, her eyes looking a little troubled.

"Charlie, why would you put things on your list that you don't really want? And don't you think that thirty is a little high? Always remember, this is just a wish list. It doesn't mean that you are getting the things you are wishing for. Sometimes Santa or the people who want to bring you something know better what might be right for you. So write a real wish list and don't expect too much. Christmas is not all about presents!"

Charlie walked to the living room, wrinkling his nose and making a grumpy face.

"What's up with you?" Noel asked.

"It's about my stupid Christmas list," Charlie huffed. "It's no fun. Mom says it shouldn't be too long and I shouldn't count on getting the stuff on it. Greg, from my soccer team, said that he is getting thirty-three presents this year. And you told me to go back and think about it. And now I don't know what to put on my list at all."

"Oh my," said Noel. "That sounds frustrating and stressful... Christmas is not about the presents, you know? – But, before you say anything, presents are sure nice to get. The person who gives them to you is saying, 'I thought about you. I wanted to give you something special. You are a wonderful part of my life.' However, if you get all worked up because you believe you will only be happy if you get all thirty gifts, you won't really enjoy anything..."

"So you're saying I shouldn't write a list at all?" Charlie looked extremely unhappy.

"No, not at all," Noel replied reassuringly. "Just don't spend so much energy on it. Don't make the joy of Christmas depend on how many presents you get or how many things you can check off your list."

"So what should I do now?" Charlie asked, still looking stressed and unsure.

"Write down ten things that would make you happy if somebody gave them to you. Then write after each thing why it would make you happy. Bring it back tomorrow."

Noel pretended to need a nap.

Charlie went to his room and started his list – again.

Family talk – December 8

1. What happens to our expectations when we have to wait a long time until they get met?
2. Further things to do: Write a Christmas list with everything you wish for the world.

December 9 – Finally Done

The next morning, before going to school, Charlie dropped his list right under Noel's nose since he seemed to still be asleep. The list read:

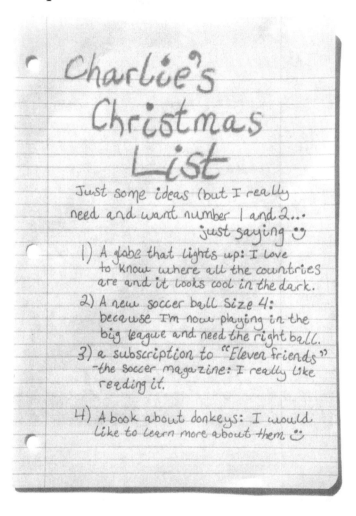

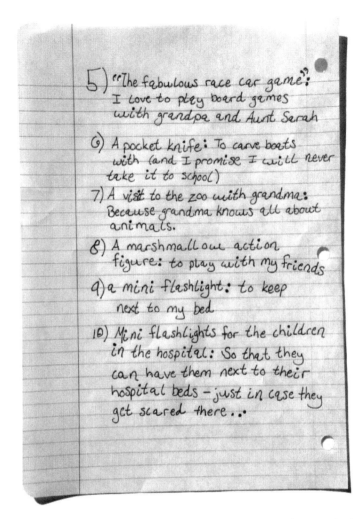

5) "The fabulous race car game": I love to play board games with grandpa and Aunt Sarah

6) A pocket knife: To carve boats with (and I promise I will never take it to school)

7) A visit to the zoo with grandma: Because grandma knows all about animals.

8) A marshmallow action figure: to play with my friends

9) a mini flashlight: to keep next to my bed

10) Mini flashlights for the children in the hospital: So that they can have them next to their hospital beds — just in case they get scared there...

When Charlie came back, he found his list next to the coat hanger. Noel had written with green marker:

I like it... especially number 4 ☺

Family talk – December 9

1. What could you add to your Christmas list that is not for you?

2. Further things to do: Write or re-write your own list.

December 10 – Making Presents

Charlie was playing with the nativity scene and telling Noel about his day at school: "My art teacher said we should make something for our parents for Christmas. He said it should be something that would be simple, that we feel would make them smile, and that shouldn't cost more than one dollar for materials. One dollar! He said he has some special money for this and if we bring in a receipt, we get one dollar back."

Charlie took a deep breath. "I have no clue what to make!"

Noel looked at Charlie somewhat amused. "Sometimes, it takes a while to get the first part of a good idea. Remember how long it took you to write your Christmas list? So, what makes them happy?"

"Well," said Charlie, "it makes my mom happy when I clean my room and it makes my dad happy when I help him in the garden."

"That's a great starting point!" said Noel. "What does your dad like to do best in the garden?"

Charlie thought hard: "He likes to plant vegetables. He likes to draw a map of the garden so all the plants are located in the right spot! You know, where each plant gets the right amount of sun and so they each have plants next to them that they really like! But right now, there is nothing growing outside…"

Noel smiled encouragingly, "A present doesn't need to be used right away. Imagine how special it is when you are surprised now and then delighted later when you pull the present out and use it."

"I know, I know!!!" Charlie was pounding on the floor with his fists he was so excited. "I can make him a bunch of those little sticks where you write down what you planted! You know, the ones that say broccoli, or basil, or anything else. That's great! He will love it. And I could put it in a little box!"

Charlie looked to Noel for agreement. "Do you think it costs less than one dollar?"

Noel nodded, "I think this is a great idea. Those sticks should be less than a dollar and the box you could make yourself, right? But you might want to think about your mom's present before spending the whole dollar...Maybe you could use rocks instead of the sticks? You could paint them and write the name of the plants on them. You can find those shiny ones at the creek and they wouldn't cost anything!"

"Yes, yes, yes! That's brilliant. Thank you Noel!" Charlie ran out of the room, grabbed his jacket, and was on his way to the creek that ran right next to his house.

Family talk – December 10

1. Come up with ideas for presents that cost nothing or very little.
2. Is it harder to make presents or to buy them? Why?
3. Further things to do: Make a gift. http://goo.gl/hDyVSz

December 11 – Acorns and Other Tiny Things

"Look at this, Noel!" Charlie came back into the living room. His pants were covered in mud and he was trying to catch his breath. But his eyes sparkled with joy!

In one hand, he held a bunch of shiny rocks, and it seemed like there were a lot more in his pockets, which were puffed out on both sides of his pants. In his other hand, he carefully showed Noel a bunch of acorns.

"Great rocks!" said Noel. "Those should work great."

"Yes," said Charlie, sounding excitedly impatient. "But look at these!" he said, holding out his pile of acorns. Noel looked at Charlie…a little lost.

"Acorns!!! For mom's fairy garden!!!!" Charlie's mom had started a small garden decorated with miniature things that she created from anything she could find in nature. In the garden, she had made a table and chairs out of twigs, a little swing, and even a miniature bird house.

Noel seemed to be slowly catching on. "So you are going to make something with the acorns for her garden?"

"Yes! I'm going to make her a tea set! It's going to be awesome! She saw one last year at the craft market and talked about it forever. The tea kettle was made of a whole acorn and the cups where made from the tops! But they also had a spout and handles made with twigs...I don't really know how to put those on."

Charlie looked discouraged now.

Noel looked at him reassuringly, "Remember Charlie, problems are there to be solved. Could your dad maybe help you or give you some tips?"

"I guess," said Charlie, nervously tapping his fingers on the door frame. "But I don't really want him to know what I'm making for mom."

"Who else do you know who might be able to help?" Noel asked, sounding positive.

"Well," Charlie thought long and hard. "Maybe my teacher could help...or...I know, maybe Mr. Grayer can help. You know, the guy who lives at the end of our street? He often sits in the park and carves little boats and stuff."

Charlie looked very hopeful now. "I'm going tomorrow after school and ask him!"

Noel tried to give Charlie a high five, but it was rather hard with a donkey's hoof. They both started to laugh.

Family talk – December 11

1. Talk about something that discourages you easily. How could you change this?

2. What would be the tiniest present you could make?

3. Further things to do: Look at this website with awesome fairy gardens http://goo.gl/Cn26cf

December 12 – All Over the World

"Did you know that my great, great, grandfather came here from Sweden?" Charlie asked Noel while he was completing the rest of his homework assignment. "Do you come from Sweden, too?"

Noel smiled and shook his head. "No, my family came from the Sahara desert. That's one reason our ears are so long."

"Huh?" Charlie looked confused.

Noel laughed, "In the desert, we are able to hear the call of another donkey 60 miles away, because of our long ears. They also help us keep cool. – I can't say that you look particularly Swedish, though. I thought they were all blond…"

Charlie shook his curly brown hair and grinned. "My dad said that they got married to people who came from all over the world. So maybe my curls are Italian."

Charlie loved to eat pizza and pasta, and considered, therefore, everything Italian to be just brilliant.

"Anyways," he said, "My granddad told me that the Swedes celebrate Lucia tomorrow. One girl in each family dresses up as Lucia. She wears a wreath with candles on her head. Can you imagine? Real candles on Isabelle's head? I mean, she's the only girl in our family. I don't think daddy would allow that."

Charlie shook his head and giggled. "The boys dress up as star boys. They have special pointy hats with stars on them. That's much cooler, don't you think?"

Noel smiled: "I remember the story of Lucia. Even though today she is mostly celebrated in Sweden, she was actually born in Italy!"

He winked at Charlie.

"Lucia was a very good person who brought food to the hungry during the long and dark winter nights. She wore a crown with candles to brighten the dark days. Many people still bake special Lucia buns and share them with neighbors and friends on Lucia day."

"Really?" asked Charlie. "I'm sure they are pretty tasty…Maybe I will go and ask mom if we could bake some tonight…"

Charlie got up from the floor. "Hey, Charlie," Noel said, "save one for me, okay?"

Charlie nodded and ran to the kitchen.

Family talk – December 12

1. Where does your family come from?
2. Do you still have relatives living abroad? Write them a Christmas card!
3. Further things to do: Bake Lucia buns!
   http://goo.gl/2evFzf
4. Make a Lucia star hat!
   http://goo.gl/4sJP8a
5. Make a Lucia paper crown.
   http://goo.gl/ItIK9g

December 13 – Lucia

Charlie's mom really liked the idea of baking Lucia buns, and they ended up making those and some ginger snaps. They also made a star hat for Charlie and a paper crown for Isabelle. Charlie could not convince his mom to put real candles on Isabelle's head, even though he promised to keep a bucket of water nearby. But they put a lot of candles on the table in the morning and had a nice Lucia breakfast.

After school, Charlie's whole family packed some treats in packages and took them to their neighbors and friends. When Charlie came home, his hands were almost frozen but he felt very good. It was so much fun to see the surprised faces of the people they delivered buns and cookies to. He carefully took one last bun out of his pocket and brought it to Noel.

"Wow, those look delicious!" said Noel, feeling a little teary eyed because Charlie had remembered to bring him a treat. "I can't wait to try it."

Charlie looked pleased and rubbed his hands to warm them up. "Um, Noel?"

Noel looked up from his bun. "Yes?"

"I saw this man standing in the toy store downtown. He was making all kinds of cool things with balloons. He could make stars, and Christmas trees, and he even had an angel. It was awesome."

"Did you get one?" asked Noel

"No," said Charlie. "We didn't go in."

"And now you are disappointed?

"Oh no, that's not it." Charlie looked hesitant. "It's just, I thought that maybe I could ask him to come with me to visit the children in the hospital and make balloons with them!" Charlie looked at the floor and then cautiously up to see

Noel's reaction.

Noel's eyes seemed once again to be filled with tears. "Oh Charlie. That is such a wonderful thought."

Charlie sighed, "But I don't know how to ask him and maybe he's already gone."

Noel shook his head, "I'm sure he is going to be there until the store closes. Maybe you could ask your mom or dad to walk there with you? I'm sure they would be happy to help!"

"Do you think they would really like that idea?" Charlie seemed unsure.

"I'm certain!" Noel looked at him proudly.

"Okay!" Charlie gathered all his strength. "I'm going to ask them! Wish me luck!"

Family talk – December 13

1. Why do we need others to help us?
2. Why is it hard sometimes to rely on others?
3. Further reading on the impact children can have:
   http://goo.gl/BFQXU7

December 14 – Balloons

Charlie's parents loved the balloon idea. Charlie was so happy this Advent season. He rarely asked when Christmas was finally going to be here, he gave his parents a Christmas list that was less than a quarter of what it was last year, and he participated enthusiastically in most Advent celebrations. He even suggested a few himself. It was because of Charlie that the family celebrated Lucia this year. And now he wanted to arrange a balloon-making session for the children in the hospital. Charlie's parents were so amazed that they secretly promised to learn how to make balloon-stars and trees if the guy from the store couldn't do it.

When Charlie took all his strength and asked the balloon maker for a session in the hospital, the balloon maker smiled. But he did hesitate awhile before answering.

"I'd love to help," he finally said. "See, Charlie – that's your name, right? – Charlie, I'm happy to come with you and make the Christmas shaped balloons. But I don't think I can afford to buy all the balloons we might need for this." Claudio, the balloon artist, looked sadly at Charlie, and Charlie's hope started to falter.

An older woman, who was looking at books in the background, pushed a few bystanders aside until she reached Charlie and Claudio. "Oh, boys," she said in a very determined tone, "no need to give up hope so easily. I'm going to pay for the balloons. Just make one tree for me, too, okay?"

Claudio, Charlie, and his parents thanked the woman over and over when more people approached. There was a woman who offered to make cookies for the event, somebody else said their sewing club would love to make some decorations, and the owner of the store promised to bring each child a little present. Charlie was amazed that all these people he had never seen before wanted to help him bring his idea to life.

The event was scheduled for the last Sunday of Advent, and the woman who promised the cookies said her brother had a very important job at the hospital and that she would arrange everything with him.

Charlie hugged his parents. He hugged Claudio and all the other people who had offered to be part of the special event. Claudio told Charlie to come back the next day, so he could teach him some techniques. Claudio wanted Charlie to be his assistant on Sunday.

When Charlie and his family walked back to their house, it started to snow. Charlie started to sing Jingle bells. His parents looked at each other smiling and joined the song. Charlie thought that he had never been happier and that this felt a lot like Christmas. "I'm so glad Christmas is not here yet," he thought. "There's still so much to look forward to before the 25th…"

Family talk – December 14

1. Think about a situation in your life where unexpectedly people showed up to help or where you helped others.
2. How does it make you feel when you can be a "helper"?
3. Further things to do: Make a "Helping hands" dove:
http://goo.gl/ahPVu0

December 15 – Family

Charlie was sitting next to Noel, showing him all the tricks Claudio has taught him when he went for his "assistant balloon artist training" after school. He could already make a flower by himself.

"I'm not sure that a flower is very Christmassy, what do you think?" He held the balloon up to Noel.

Noel wrinkled his nose, "I think flowers can be very festive. Think of the Poinsettia!"

Charlie jumped up as if he remembered something extremely important and ran into the kitchen. A little later he came back, carefully carrying the vase with the cherry branches. "Look at this, Noel! Can you see it?" He placed the vase right next to Noel.

Noel shook his head, "I can't see anything…well, besides some branches in a beautiful vase, of course."

"Don't you remember?" said Charlie.

"Those are the Barbara branches. And the first leaf is sprouting out!"

He pointed to the little green tip and Noel smiled contently.

"Advent is for sure moving along," he said. "Not much longer and it's going to be Christmas! Are you excited, Charlie?"

"Yes!" said Charlie. "But I'm really glad it's not going to be tomorrow because I have a lot to do before it comes. Tomorrow I'm meeting with Mrs. Grayer to work on the tea set for mom. I thought that Mr. Grayer could help me, but when I asked him, he said that his wife does tiny crafts all the time. She seemed really happy to help me. She even said we could make a little vase with flowers. Mom will be so excited! – Hey, Noel, do you have a Christmas list?"

Noel shook his head. "Not really. But I'd sure like some tasty treats if anybody asks." He winked at Charlie.

"I thought donkeys eat hey and grass," Charlie replied.

"Well," Noel blushed a little, "yes, that's true but that doesn't mean we don't like something sweet once in a while…"

"Are you going to celebrate Christmas with your family?" asked Charlie.

"I thought I'm part of your family, now," replied Noel.

Charlie smiled, "So that's a yes?"

"That's a yes!" Noel said.

Family talk – December 15

1. Who do you count as family?
2. How is your Barbara branch doing?
3. Further things to do: Learn something about your family's history
   http://goo.gl/sQQCro
4. Research the Poinsettia and why it's considered the Christmas flower
   http://goo.gl/jlBtY3

December 16 – The Star Child

Everything was going great. Charlie felt like he was on top of the world. Nothing could stop him now. Or so he thought.

On Monday, Charlie woke up not feeling well. When he finally managed to put his clothes on and go downstairs to the kitchen, his dad took one look at him and carried him straight back to bed. His mom brought him some tea and took his temperature. They said Charlie had to stay in his bed for a few days. Charlie felt miserable. He couldn't go and work with Mrs. Grayer and he was worried that he might not be fully recovered for Sunday's event.

"Is there anything else I can bring you, Charlie?" asked his mom.

Charlie nodded his head. His throat felt really sore and it was hard for him to speak: "Could you bring Noel up?"

"The donkey?" his mom asked. Charlie nodded again. "Sure thing," she said and went to the living room and brought up Noel.

It made Charlie feel a little better to have some company. Even though Isabelle often got on his nerves, he missed having her around now that his parents said it would be better for his sister not to visit him in his room.

Noel gave him a compassionate look, "Should I sing something for you?" he asked.

Charlie got out a little giggle, "No offense, but donkeys are not really known for their singing...Could you tell me a story?"

Noel pretended to be a little offended but turned around pretty fast to start his story:

"Once upon a time there was a little girl who was all alone. She had nothing else but the clothes she was wearing and a little piece of bread. She was a very good and faithful girl, and even though it seemed that the world had forsaken her, she trusted that God had something good in store for her. It was Christmas Eve when the girl walked into the country, not knowing where God would lead her.

"She met a poor shepherd who asked her for something to eat. She reached into her pocket, gave the man her bread and said, 'When Jesus was born, you ran to greet him. I wish I could greet you with more than this, but it's all I have.' And she went on her way.

"Then came a child who had just finished cleaning the little stable his family owned. The child was shivering and the girl took off her cape, gave it to him and said, 'Jesus was born in a stable like this, because a kind family gave Mary and Joseph a place to stay. I wish I could cover you with more than this, but it's all I have.' And she went on her way.

"When she walked a little farther, she met two other children who were herding an ox and a donkey and who were freezing cold. So the girl gave them her jacket and dress, 'An ox and a donkey watched over Jesus when he was born. I wish I could protect you better, but it's all I have.'

"Now the girl had only her undershirt left and she went into the forest to hide. And as she so stood and had nothing left, she suddenly saw a fir tree covered with stars. When she got closer, she saw that the stars were made of pure gold. She gathered all of the gold into her shirt and was rich all the days of her life."

When Noel looked up, Charlie was fast asleep.

"Sleep tight, Charlie. I hope you feel better soon!"

Family talk – December 16

1. What cheers you up when you are ill?
2. What do you do for others when they are not feeling well?
3. Further things to do: Donate something to Goodwill.
4. Make a "get well" card for somebody who is not feeling too good.
   http://goo.gl/mMVICo

December 17 – Advent Calendars

Charlie didn't feel better the next day. He actually felt worse. His grandma came to read stories to Charlie and brought him his favorite soup. His grandpa told him stories of all the pranks he played as a little boy – which were by far Charlie's favorite stories. But the fever still kept him weak and his mom said he needed to stay in bed. She did bring the Barbara branch up so Charlie could see that two more leaves were coming out, and she moved the chocolate Advent calendar into Charlie's room. But Charlie didn't even feel like chocolate. He offered the piece of the day to Noel. Noel was touched.

"That's very sweet of you, Charlie. But I think you should save it for tomorrow. I'm sure you will appreciate an extra piece of chocolate...," he smiled. "Did you know that children have had Advent calendars for a long time?"

Charlie shook his head.

Noel cleared his throat. "A long time ago, the Advent calendar was thought of as something to help children shorten the time until Christmas. Over the years, the look of the calendar changed quite a bit. Depending on the country, some had 24 doors. Some had 25. Many people have their Christmas celebration on Christmas Eve.

"Anyways, even people in the 17th century had something resembling an Advent calendar. Some families put up a new religious picture each day, others painted 25 chalk strokes on the living room door and each day a child could erase one. Others set up the nativity scene without baby Jesus and put one piece of hay into the manger on each day."

Charlie looked up. "I think I like chocolate better."

Noel laughed, "Well, there is magic in

each of those, don't you think? And it also shows you that children always had a hard time waiting for Christmas."

"I have a hard time waiting to not be sick anymore," Charlie grumbled. "Could we make a calendar for that?"

"We sure can," Noel answered. "How many more cups of chamomile tea do you think you need to drink until you feel better?"

Noel stopped talking when Charlie's mom came in. "Mom," asked Charlie, "How many cups of tea do you think I need to drink until I feel all better?"

His mom looked at him curiously. "Well, you never really know, but I think twenty should do it!"

"Okay," Charlie nodded, "could you make 20 chalk strokes on my door and wipe one off every time I finish a cup?"

His mom raised her eyebrow, smiled and shook her head.

"I'll get you another cup of tea right now!"

Family talk – December 17

1. Do you have an Advent calendar? Does it make waiting easier?
2. What other Advent traditions does your family have? Which ones did you notice at other families you know?
3. Further things to do: Research Advent traditions
http://goo.gl/cBE6ko

December 18 – Helping Hands

Charlie felt better the next day even though he still had thirteen cups of tea left to drink. But he felt strong enough to play a game of memory with his dad, and grandpa taught him a new card trick.

His dad came up to Charlie's room in the afternoon. "Charlie," he said in a surprised tone, "Mrs. Grayer is here to see you. She said you wanted to help her with a project?"

"Oh yes," Charlie blushed. "Yes, dad, can she please come up?"

"I'm already up!" he heard Mrs. Grayer from the door. "You know Charlie, I thought that it might be a good distraction for you if we could work together on my project."

She winked at him.

"Thank you so much," said his dad. "That's really very kind of you. Can I bring you anything?"

"I think we are good," said Mrs. Grayer.

When Charlie's dad was gone, Mrs. Grayer pulled a tray out of her bag which she put on Charlie's bed. Next came a box with all kinds of tools. "Where are the acorns?" she asked Charlie.

"Oh," he replied, "they are over in my desk drawer. I can get them."

Mrs. Grayer shook her head, "No, you need to rest. I'll get them for you."

She got the acorns out and the two of them started working on the acorn tea set. Charlie was amazed. He had no idea that this project would turn out so beautiful.

"Thank you so much, Mrs. Grayer!" he whispered.

"Thank _you_, Charlie. It's been a while since I could share this craft with somebody else! Do you want me to take this tea set home until Christmas so your mom doesn't see it?"

"Yes," said Charlie, "That would probably be best. Thank you again."

His dad came in just when Mrs. Grayer had everything carefully packed away.

"I'm on my way," she said. "Thanks for all your help, Charlie!" She winked again. Charlie smiled back and waved.

Charlie's dad came back a little later to bring another cup of tea and some crackers. "So," he asked, "what was that all about?"

Charlie snuggled back into his pillow, "It's Christmas time, daddy. Everybody has their surprises, you know?"

Family talk – December 18

Have some tea with your family while you talk…

1. How hard is it for you to keep surprises?
2. What was the best surprise you ever had?
3. Further things to do: Learn how to draw a donkey.

   http://goo.gl/SqE5zM

December 19 – Snow

When Charlie woke up there was snow outside his window. The flakes were falling slowly as if they were gently dancing downwards, taking their sweet time.

His dad peeked into his room. "Good morning, Charlie!" He smiled. "You look much better today!"

Charlie smiled back: "I am. I'm all better!"

His dad come closer and put his hands on Charlie's forehead: "It looks like the fever has broken. That's great. Now we have to make sure you take it easy for a couple of days so you recover fully!"

Charlie wrinkled his forehead. He thought he could jump right back in, but then he looked at the door and saw that there were still seven chalk stripes up there.

"Can I come down for breakfast today, daddy?"

His dad nodded.

"And can I have pancakes? With cinnamon? And can I have two cups of tea?"

Charlie kept asking questions while he got out of bed and followed his dad down the stairs. He hugged Isabelle for a long time until she started to get impatient with him and wiggled free.

His mom let Charlie stay downstairs for a while as long as he promised to take it easy. She took out a stack of Christmas cards and told Charlie to write his name on each. Charlie asked who each card was for. If it was somebody he knew, he put the card in a separate stack.

"What are you doing?" his mom asked.

Charlie answered, "I want to draw a little picture for these people. I think it would make them happy!"

"That's a great idea Charlie," replied his mom. "What are you going to draw?"

"A donkey!" said Charlie without hesitation.

His mom smiled and wondered, once more, how and why the stuffed donkey that Charlie didn't even look twice at last year had become such a dear friend. She helped Charlie find a tutorial on how to draw donkeys and Charlie spent the whole morning working on his drawings. He even let Isabelle add her special toddler art to it. Charlie took a long nap after lunch. When he woke up, he wanted to go outside to play in the snow but his parents said that he needed to wait until tomorrow. So Charlie sat behind the window, watching the snow and the children playing in it with longing.

"Did you know that each snowflake is unique?" asked Noel. "They all look differently but we can only see that when we look at them under a microscope!"

Charlie looked up. "Dad has a microscope!" he opened his door to call his dad. "I'll ask him if we can set it up here so you can look at the snowflakes with us!"

Family talk – December 19

1. Take your talk outside and talk while you walk. Discuss the beauty of nature around you. You might have snow right now, or maybe it's mild where you live. Point out whatever beauty you see.
2. Further things to do: Make a snowflake
http://goo.gl/7zRfy8

December 20 – Part of Something Great

Charlie practically fell into his snowsuit and boots the next morning. He took very little time to eat because he wanted to play in the snow as soon as possible. The neighbor kids were already gathering. The group spent the whole morning building snow animals and having snow fights. Charlie's cheeks and nose were bright red when he came in for lunch but his smile filled his face.

"Can I go outside again after lunch?" he asked.

His mom studied him for a while. "After you take a nap!" she said.

"But mom," Charlie answered, "naps are for babies!"

"And for kids who are still recovering from being sick!"

His mom's tone told Charlie that there was no point in arguing. He finished lunch and went to his room.

It looked like Noel was looking at a book. Charlie looked closer and recognized his children's Bible. "What are you reading?" he asked Noel.

"I was looking up the story with the donkey. I mean," he blushed and corrected himself, "the story where the donkey carried Mary all the way from Nazareth to Bethlehem. The Bible tells us that the Roman Emperor Augustus wanted to have a list of all the people in the empire, to make sure they paid their taxes. He ordered everyone to return to the town where their families came from, and to enter their names in a register there. Mary and Joseph travelled a long way - about 70 miles - from Nazareth to Bethlehem, because that is where Joseph's family came from. Most people walked but some lucky people had a donkey to help carry the goods needed for the journey. Joseph and Mary travelled very slowly because Mary was going to have a baby, and it was going to be born soon."

Noel paused for a moment. When he continued, he said, "You know, I thought about this because it's just somehow amazing to be part of it – or even to have one of your great, great, great, great grandfathers or mothers be part of it. It has changed how people look at donkeys today."

"Do you think that it's true for people, too?" Charlie wondered. "Do you think that if God helps one person to do something great or be part of something great, that it changes everybody?"

"Wow, Charlie," answered Noel. "Those are big questions. "But I really do believe so. I believe that whenever somebody plays his or her part in God's story, people can see what's possible and that might inspire them. And we so often see that during Advent and Christmas, don't we? It's often the little things but don't underestimate them. Many little waves can move the water, sometimes with more force than one big wave."

Family talk – December 20

1. Do you think that if God helps one person to do something great or be part of something great, that it changes everybody?
2. Further things to do: Make a frozen sun catcher
   http://goo.gl/6YBAO5

December 21 – Stone Soup

Charlie spent most of Saturday with Claudio in the toy shop watching him make all kinds of shapes out of balloons. Whenever Claudio had a break, he would practice with Charlie. Charlie made notes of all the steps that were needed to make stars and Christmas trees. When he got home, he typed them on the computer with his dad and they printed them out so they could give them to all the kids in the hospital.

Once he was done, Charlie went to his room and pulled out the bag of rocks he had gathered for his dad's present. He washed them in the sink and dried them gently. Then he took out all the paint he had, covered his desk with an old newspaper, and started to paint each rock. He smiled as he watched the pile of rocks look more and more like rainbow colored gems. Charlie had to wait for the paint to dry before he could write all the plant names on them, so he turned to

Noel to show him his work.

Noel inspected the rocks and nodded approvingly. "I love how colorful they are," he said. "It's amazing how you can turn something as simple as a rock into something so much more just by adding a few things. It reminds me of the story of stone soup."

Charlie looked up, "Can you tell it to me, pleeaaase?"

He gave Noel a long look to try to get him to tell the story. Charlie loved Noel's stories.

Noel cleared his throat and started the story: "A group of travelers came to a village, carrying an empty pot. They asked for food but nobody was willing to share with them. So they filled the pot with water, dropped a large stone into it and placed it over a fire. One of the villagers became curious and asked what they were doing. The travelers answered that they were making 'stone soup,' which would taste wonderful once done, but they needed a little more garnish to improve the flavor. The villager had never heard of stone soup and was only too willing to help them out with a few carrots which they added to the pot. Other villagers walked by and one by one they contributed some ingredients to the soup. By the end of the day, a delicious soup was enjoyed by all."

Charlie drummed with his fingers on the table. "You know," he said to Noel, "we did this once at soccer practice. Ms. Loger brought a white flag and said this was going to be our team flag. She said she really liked it, but if we wanted, we could bring something next week and could add it to it. It was really funny. I brought a stamp that looks like a soccer ball and we stamped all around the flag with it. Ben brought a little felt bear that looked like our mascot and his mom helped to sew it on, and Olivia brought a lot of glitter....girls," he rolled his eyes and laughed at Noel. "I think my rocks are ready for the next step!"

Family talk – December 21

1. Did you ever see somebody start with nothing yet create something great?
2. What lessons can we learn from stories like this?
3. Further things to do: Bring some food items to your local food pantry.

December 22 – The Big Event

Charlie was up at six in the morning because he was so nervous. The balloon session wouldn't start until the afternoon, but to Charlie it felt longer to wait for this than to wait for Christmas. Finally, his parents said to get in the car, and they all drove to the hospital.

The sewing group had done a great job decorating. They had put up long tables for everybody to sit on and had made special tablecloths. Little nativity scenes served as center pieces, and there were many plates with cookies and fruit. A little table at the side had water and hot apple cider on it. Instead of paper cups, there was a mug for each kid and somebody had written each kid's name on them. There was even one for Charlie and one for Isabelle.

Claudio came in and set up his balloon making table on a little podium so that everybody could see him. Finally, it was time, and almost 30 children were brought to the room. Some came in in wheelchairs or on crutches and a couple had to carry oxygen tanks.

Charlie's parents were glad they had prepared their children for the hospital, and so Charlie didn't seem too scared or shy at all. He tried to go to each of child and wish them 'Happy Christmas' – but he added right away that it was not really Christmas yet but that this was just something that was nice to say.

After a first round of cookies and cider, the kids got their yellow balloons to make stars. After demonstrating it a couple of times, Claudio, Charlie, and Charlie's parents went around the room and helped where help was needed. A couple of nurses and the woman who bought the balloons also pitched in. Everybody was having a good time. The second project was more complicated and Claudio tried to explain each step very slowly so the kids would be able to make their own balloon tree. Halfway through his presentation a little girl stood up and raised her hand.

"Mr. Balloon guy," she said, "could we make instead one big tree? We could all put our balloons together and we could have a big tree in the cafeteria where we always go to eat!"

Everybody stared at the girl for a couple of seconds but then the kids started to cheer. Claudio took a piece of paper and tried to sketch something down.

When the group quieted down, he said, "Let's give it a try. I have never done this before but it sure sounds wonderful. I'm wondering how we can make it stand up."

One of the doctors who was watching the crafting session went back into his room and brought a tall coat tree.

Claudio smiled, "that should do it."

It took much longer than anticipated, and some of the kids needed to go back to their rooms early because they didn't have the energy to stay up for too long. But by the end of the afternoon, they had created a big standing balloon tree. The kids cheered again.

"How about a song?" one of the nurses called.

And the whole room started to sing "Oh Christmas Tree." Some of the kids and adults had tears running down their cheeks. Charlie was holding his mom's hand very tight.

"I know it's not Christmas," he thought, "but I think you can only feel this Christmassy when it's getting close."

Family talk – December 22

1. Why is it sometimes more fun to make something big with many people than something little just by yourself?
2. What are situations where you enjoy working by yourself?
3. Further things to do: Sing Christmas songs

December 23 – Christingles

Every year on the 23rd, Charlie's grandmother came over to make Christingles for family and friends. Charlie was never very interested in this before, but a lot had changed this time. He was curious as to what this was all about, and he was actually looking forward to spending some time with his grandma.

His grandmother brought a box filled with oranges, candles, and other supplies to the house and she, Charlie's mom, and his aunt gathered around the kitchen table to set everything up. Charlie was watching from the door.

"Do you want to join us, Charlie?" his grandma asked.

"Sure," Charlie replied as casual as he could.

The three women smiled knowingly. They saw how Charlie had changed during the last three weeks and were not surprised to find him interested in this tradition.

"Let me tell you all about Christingles," his grandma started. "It's a tradition that apparently comes from the Czech Republic. I wish I had a map to show you where that is…"

"Maybe we can look it up in daddy's atlas, "Charlie said happily, "after we are done, of course!"

His grandma nodded and continued with the story: "It is told that a poor family couldn't bring a present to church on Christmas Eve as it was the custom to do there, but they found an orange, which they thought would make a nice gift. However, they discovered that the orange was getting moldy and they had to cut off the top. They thought that maybe they could make a lantern out of the orange. So they put a candle in it and tied a red ribbon around it. The ribbon didn't want to stay in place so they fastened it with four little sticks and decorated those with raisins. They took the lantern to church, nervous about how the others would respond. But the priest picked up the lantern and explained to the church why it was so special:

'The orange is round like the world.

'The candle stands tall and straight and gives light in the dark like the love of God.

'The red ribbon goes all around the 'world' and is a symbol of the blood Jesus shed when he died for us.

'The four sticks point in all directions and symbolize North, South, East and West - they also represent the four seasons.

'The fruit represent the fruits of the earth, nurtured by the sunshine and the rain.'

"And this is how people started making Christingles for Christmas!"

Charlie's grandma looked at Charlie, "So, are you ready to help us make some?"

Charlie nodded his head eagerly, "Yes, I am," he said. "And grandma, can I make one for Mrs. Grayer, too?"

His grandma winked at him. "Sure thing, make one for whomever you can think of!"

And Charlie got to work.

Family talk – December 23

1. Discuss and explain all the different things the Christingle symbolizes.
2. Further things to do: Make a Christingle.

December 24 – Marshmallow Figures

It was Christmas Eve morning. Charlie entered the kitchen to cinnamon rolls and hot chocolate. His dad was taking down the Advent wreath that had been sitting on the table for the last four weeks and Charlie felt a little sad that this wonderful Advent season was coming to an end. But then he caught a glimpse of the Christmas tree and got excited for Christmas.

After breakfast, Charlie's dad took him to the side, "Charlie, I just wanted to talk to you about something."

Charlie looked nervous, and his dad was quick to calm him down, "No, no, you didn't do anything wrong," he gave Charlie an encouraging look. "It's just that I got a note from Santa. He told me that many kids this year have asked for a marshmallow action figure, and he wasn't sure if there would be enough for everybody to get one. So just in case you don't find one under the tree, there is still a chance that you might get it for your birthday in February, okay?"

Charlie shrugged with his shoulders. "It's not a big deal, really dad."

His dad look confused and relieved, "Okay, Charlie. Would you make sure the nativity scene is set up properly?"

Noel had found his way back under the tree and Charlie sat next to him to make sure everything in and around the little wooden stable looked neat. He told Noel about the marshmallow figure.

"You don't seem very disappointed," said Noel.

"I'm really not," Charlie replied. "I'm actually a little relieved, you know?"

Noel shook his head.

"Well," Charlie continued, "I was never really too thrilled with them but everybody was talking about them, so I thought I needed to have one too. But then, when I redid my list, I put it near the bottom, hoping Santa would see the other stuff before it. Maybe I was a bit of a coward to not just take it off my list, but I was hoping that this way I wouldn't necessarily get it and then I could just tell the others it was Santa's fault..."

Charlie looked anxiously at Noel, not knowing if he should be proud of this strategy or embarrassed.

Noel smiled and said, "You know, Charlie, I think Santa might have known all along that this was not what would make Christmas this year special for you. So, I don't think you have to worry too much about it!"

Charlie smiled gratefully and said, "Well, I won't. But I _will_ make sure that I don't put anything like that on my list next year."

Family talk – December 24

1. Think of situations where you used a strategy to get your point across without saying it out loud.
2. Further things to do: Set the breakfast table for Christmas day.

December 25 – Happy Noel

Charlie woke up early on Christmas day. He went to get Isabelle and they jumped onto their parent's bed.

"Happy Christmas!" Charlie called. "Let's all get up and go down to the living room!"

His parents laughed and they marched in their pajamas down the stairs. Before opening the door, Charlie's dad took out a Bible and read to them:

"In those days, Caesar Augustus made a law. It required that a list be made of everyone in the whole Roman world. It was the first time a list was made of the people while Quirinius was governor of Syria. All went to their own towns to be listed.

"So Joseph went also. He went from the town of Nazareth in Galilee to Judea. That is where Bethlehem, the town of David, was. Joseph went there because he belonged to the family line of David. He went there with Mary to be listed. Mary was engaged to him. She was expecting a baby.

"While Joseph and Mary were there, the time came for the child to be born. She gave birth to her first baby. It was a boy. She wrapped him in large strips of cloth. Then she placed him in a manger. There was no room for them in the inn."

Charlie's mom came in with a cake and they all sang "Happy Birthday, Jesus" as they had done every year before. "Cake or presents first?" his mom asked.

Charlie and Isabelle laughed, "Presents!"

They opened the living room door and stood for a moment in awe, looking at the room that was so festive and so filled with wonder. Charlie saw that his mom had moved the Barbara branches onto the side table, and it sure looked like one of the flowers was blossoming.

"Which one would you like to open first, Charlie?" his dad asked.

"I'll pick one in a moment," said Charlie.

He took a red ribbon out from behind the tree where he had hidden it last night. He tied it around Noel's neck, put a bowl of cookies in front of him, and hugged him tight.

"Merry Christmas, Noel!" he whispered. "And thank you!"

Charlie knew that Noel wouldn't talk while anybody else was in the room, but he saw a little sparkling shimmer in the donkey's eyes.

About the Author

 Franziska Macur is a mom of two little girls. She homeschools by day and writes and blogs in the wee hours. She is a certified Simplicity Parenting group leader and is always looking for simplicity, rhythm, creativity, wholesomeness, and an overall natural lifestyle...

Franziska has a Ph.D. in Communication Studies from the University of Bonn. She left the tenure-track life of higher education to be a stay-at-home mom to her two young, bilingual daughters.

For more information about Franziska, go to **www.homenaturally.org**

CPSIA information can be obtained at www.ICGtesting.com
Printed in the USA
LVOW07s0044291114

416153LV00001B/119/P